Margery Williams's

THE VELVETEEN RABBIT

Or How Toys Become Real

adaptation *by* Lou Fancher
paintings *by* Steve Johnson *and* Lou Fancher

An Anne Schwartz Book
ATHENEUM BOOKS FOR YOUNG READERS
New York London Toronto Sydney Simgapore

There was once a velveteen rabbit, and in the beginning he was really splendid. On Christmas morning, he sat wedged in the top of the Boy's stocking.

There were other things in the stocking, but the Rabbit was quite the best of all. For at least two hours the Boy loved him, and then the Velveteen Rabbit was forgotten.

For a long time the Rabbit lived in the toy cupboard or on the nursery floor. He was naturally shy, and being only made of velveteen, some of the more expensive toys quite snubbed him. Even Timothy, the jointed wooden lion, put on airs. The only person who was kind to him was the Skin Horse.

The Skin Horse was old and wise, and he knew all about being Real.

"What is REAL?" asked the Rabbit one day. "Does it mean having things that buzz inside you and a stick-out handle?"

"Real isn't how you are made," said the Skin Horse. "When a child loves you for a long, long time, not just to play with, but REALLY loves you, then you become Real."

"Does it hurt?" asked the Rabbit.

"Sometimes," said the Skin Horse. "When you are Real you don't mind being hurt."

"Does it happen all at once," he asked, "like being wound up?"

"It doesn't happen all at once," said the Skin Horse. "By the time you are Real, most of your hair has been loved off, and you get very shabby. But once you are Real you can't become unreal again. It lasts for always."

The Rabbit sighed. He thought it would be a long time before this magic called Real happened to him.

There was a person called Nana who ruled the nursery. Sometimes, for no reason whatever, she went swooping about like a great wind and hustled the toys away in cupboards. She called this "tidying up."

One evening, when the Boy was going to bed, he couldn't find the china dog that always slept with him.

"Here," Nana said, "take your old Bunny!" And she dragged the Rabbit out by one ear, and put him into the Boy's arms.

That night, and for many nights after, the Velveteen Rabbit slept in the Boy's bed. Soon, he grew to like it, for the Boy made nice tunnels for him under the bedclothes that he said were like the burrow the real rabbits lived in. When the Boy dropped off to sleep, the Rabbit would snuggle close all night long.

And so, the little Rabbit was happy—so happy that he never noticed how his fur was getting shabbier and all the pink had rubbed off his nose where the boy had kissed him.

Spring came, and wherever the Boy went, the Rabbit went too. Once, the Rabbit was left out on the lawn and Nana had to look for him because the Boy couldn't go to sleep unless he was there.

"Fancy all that fuss for a toy!" she said.

"Give me my Bunny!" he said. "He isn't a toy. He's REAL!"

When the little Rabbit heard that, he knew the nursery magic had happened to him. He was Real.

That night, so much love stirred in his little sawdust heart that it almost burst.

Near the house there was a wood, where the Boy liked to play. One evening, while the Rabbit was lying there alone, he saw two strange beings.

They were rabbits like himself, but they changed shape when they moved, instead of always staying the same like he did.

They stared at him, and the little Rabbit stared back. Their noses twitched.

"Why don't you get up and play with us?" one of them asked.

"I don't feel like it," said the Rabbit.

"Ho!" said the furry rabbit, and he gave a big hop sideways. "I don't believe you can!"

"I can!" said the little Rabbit. "I can jump higher than anything." He meant when the Boy threw him, but of course he didn't want to say so.

"Can you hop on your hind legs?" asked the furry rabbit.

That was a dreadful question, for the Velveteen Rabbit had no hind legs at all! He sat still and hoped that the rabbit wouldn't notice.

But the rabbit looked.

"He hasn't got any hind legs," he called out.

"I have!" cried the little Rabbit. "I am sitting on them."

"Then stretch them out and show me, like this!" said the wild rabbit. And he began to whirl around and dance.

"I don't like dancing," the little Rabbit said.

But all the while he was longing to dance.

The strange rabbit came quite close. He wrinkled his nose.

"He doesn't smell right!" he exclaimed. "He isn't a rabbit at all! He isn't real!"

"I *am* Real!" said the little Rabbit. "The Boy said so!" And he nearly began to cry.

Just then the Boy ran near them, and with a flash of white tails the two strange rabbits disappeared.

"Oh do come back and play with me!" called the little Rabbit. "I *know* I am Real!"

But there was no answer.

Weeks passed, and the little Rabbit grew very old and shabby, but the Boy loved him just as much.

And then, one day, the Boy was ill. Strange people came and went in the nursery. Through it all the little Rabbit lay there, and never stirred, afraid that someone might take him away. He knew that the Boy needed him.

Presently the fever turned, and the Boy got better. One day, they let him get up and dress. He was going to the seaside.

"Hurrah!" thought the little Rabbit, for he wanted to see the big waves, and the tiny crabs, and the sand castles.

Just then Nana caught sight of him.
"How about his old Bunny?" she asked.

"*That?*" said the doctor. "Why, it's a mass of scarlet fever germs! Burn it at once."

And so the little Rabbit was put into a sack and carried out to the end of the garden. The gardener promised to come early the next morning and burn the whole lot.

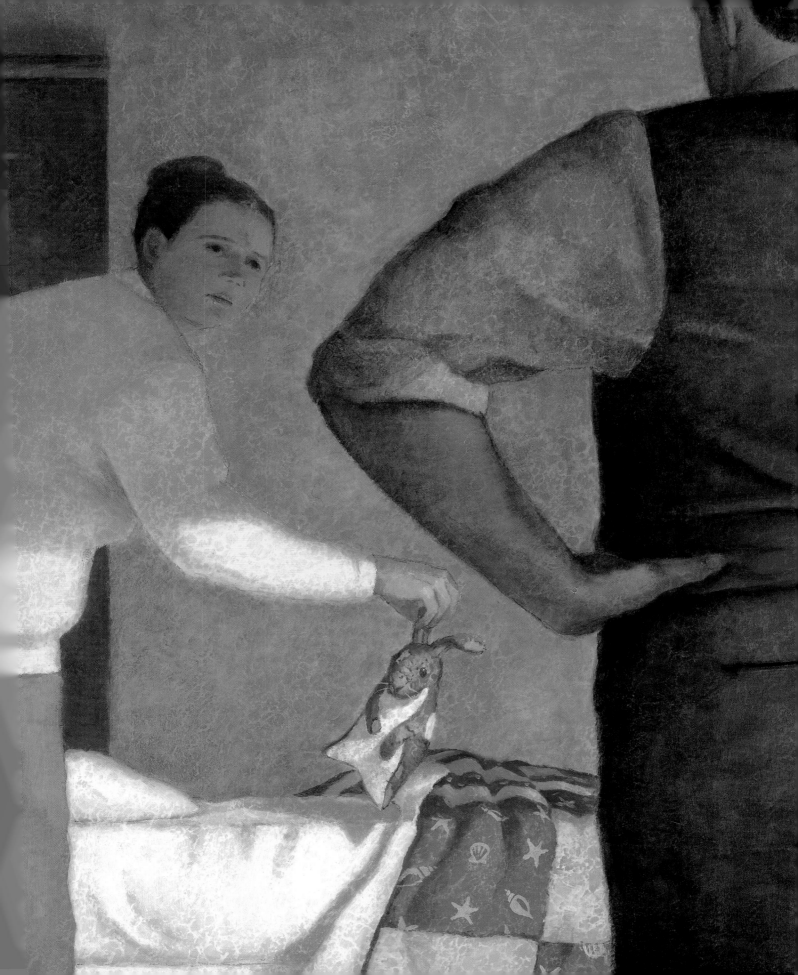

The little Rabbit felt very lonely. He thought of those long sunlit hours in the garden, and a great sadness came over him. What use was it to become Real if it all ended like this? A tear, a real tear, trickled down his little shabby velvet nose and fell to the ground.

And then a strange thing happened. For where the tear had fallen, a flower grew out of the ground, and out of it there stepped a fairy.

"Little Rabbit," she said, "don't you know who I am?"

The Rabbit looked up at her, and it seemed to him that he had seen her face before.

"I am the nursery magic Fairy," she said. "I take care of all the playthings that the children have loved. I turn them into Real."

"Wasn't I Real before?" asked the little Rabbit.

"You were Real to the Boy," the Fairy said, "because he loved you. Now you shall be Real to everyone."

And she held the little Rabbit close and flew with him into the wood. In the open glade between the tree trunks, she kissed him and put him down on the grass.

"Run and play, little Rabbit!" she said.

But the little Rabbit sat quite still. For he suddenly remembered that he was made all in one piece. He did not know that when the Fairy kissed him, she had changed him altogether. And he might have sat there a long time, if something hadn't tickled his nose. He lifted his hind toe to scratch it.

He actually had hind legs! He gave one leap, and the joy of using those hind legs was so great that he went springing about the turf.

He was a Real Rabbit at last.

Autumn passed and Winter, and in the Spring the Boy went out to play. And while he was playing, a rabbit peeped at him.

"Why, he looks just like my old Bunny that was lost when I had scarlet fever!"

But he never knew that it really was his own Bunny, come back to look at the child who had first helped him to be Real.

A Note to the Reader

The idea of adapting Margery Williams's *The Velveteen Rabbit* for a younger audience came to me soon after my child arrived. Wanting to introduce him to classic tales, I found myself "adapting" longer stories for a wiggly two-year-old. I had the pleasure of revisiting childhood favorites and my son learned early on to love good books.

At almost the same time, my husband and I were completing paintings for *Bambi*, adapted by Janet Schulman. I admired the way Janet had retained the beauty of Felix Salten's original story, while telling it in fewer words.

In creating this picture book version of *The Velveteen Rabbit,* I've shortened the text to allow more room for the artwork. In doing so, I've preserved as much of the original language as possible. Occasionally, for clarity, I have made minor alterations. I hope that young children who love this book will read and enjoy the original when they are older.

FOR NICHOLAS

Atheneum Books for Young Readers
An imprint of Simon & Schuster Children's Publishing Division
1230 Avenue of the Americas, New York, New York 10020

Book design by Lou Fancher
The text of this book is set in Souvenir.
The paintings are rendered in oil on paper.

Printed in Hong Kong
2 4 6 8 10 9 7 5 3 1
Library of Congress Cataloging-in-Publication Data
Fancher, Lou.
The velveteen rabbit / adapted by Lou Fancher from the original story by Margery Williams :
illustrations by Steve Johnson and Lou Fancher.
p.   cm.
"An Anne Schwartz Book."
Summary: By the time the Velveteen Rabbit is dirty, worn out, and about to be burned, he has almost
given up hope of ever finding the magic called Real.
ISBN 0-689-84134-5
[1. Toys—Fiction. 2. Rabbits—Fiction.] I. Johnson, Steve, 1960– ill. II. Fancher, Lou, 1960– ill.
III. Bianco, Margery Williams, 1880–1944. Velveteen Rabbit. IV. Title.
PZ7.F1988 Ve 2002
[E]—dc21
2001022675

FIRST
EDITION